TOTALLY TARDY
MARTY

words by
Erica S. Perl

pictures by
Jarrett J. Krosoczka

ABRAMS BOOKS FOR YOUNG READERS
New York

To the real—life Marty and Kate, who may or may not be related to me
—ESP

For Simone and Zelda
—JJK

THE ILLUSTRATIONS IN THIS BOOK WERE MADE WITH PEN, INK, WATERCOLOR, AND ACRYLICS DIGITALLY COLLAGED.

Library of Congress Cataloging-in-Publication Data: Perl, Erica S. Totally Tardy Marty / by Erica S. Perl ; illustrated by Jarrett J. Krosoczka. pages cm. ISBN 978-1-4197-1661-4 [1. Tardiness—Fiction. 2. Punctuality—Fiction. 3. Friendship—Fiction.] I. Krosoczka, Jarrett J., illustrator. II. Title. PZ7.P3163Tot 2015 [E]—dc23 2014040136

Text copyright © 2015 Erica S. Perl · Illustrations copyright © 2015 Jarrett J. Krosoczka · Book design by Chad W. Beckerman

Abrams Books for Young Readers are available at special discounts when purchased in quantity for premiums and promotions as well as fundraising or educational use. Special editions can also be created to specification. For details, contact specialsales@abramsbooks.com or the address below.

ABRAMS
THE ART OF BOOKS SINCE 1949
115 West 18th Street
New York, NY 10011
www.abramsbooks.com

On Monday, Marty was just about to leave for school when an idea hit him like a ton of toast. There was no time to waste—this could revolutionize breakfast!

Like all great ideas, it needed
a little fine-tuning.
But finally:

BEHOLD...
Toast-on-
a-Rope!

UH-OH.

Tuesday morning was pretty quiet. Maybe too quiet . . .
Quiet like the quiet before . . . a giant squid attack!!!

It was Never-Late Kate.

Never-Late Kate who thought she was sooo great.

So, Marty was tardy. Totally tardy.

TOTALLY TARDY MARTY.

On Wednesday morning, no toast, no squid attack, no nothing.

But when Marty walked out the door . . .

It was Never-Late Kate.

Never-Late Kate who thought she was sooo great.

But then . . .

In a flash, Kate was back.

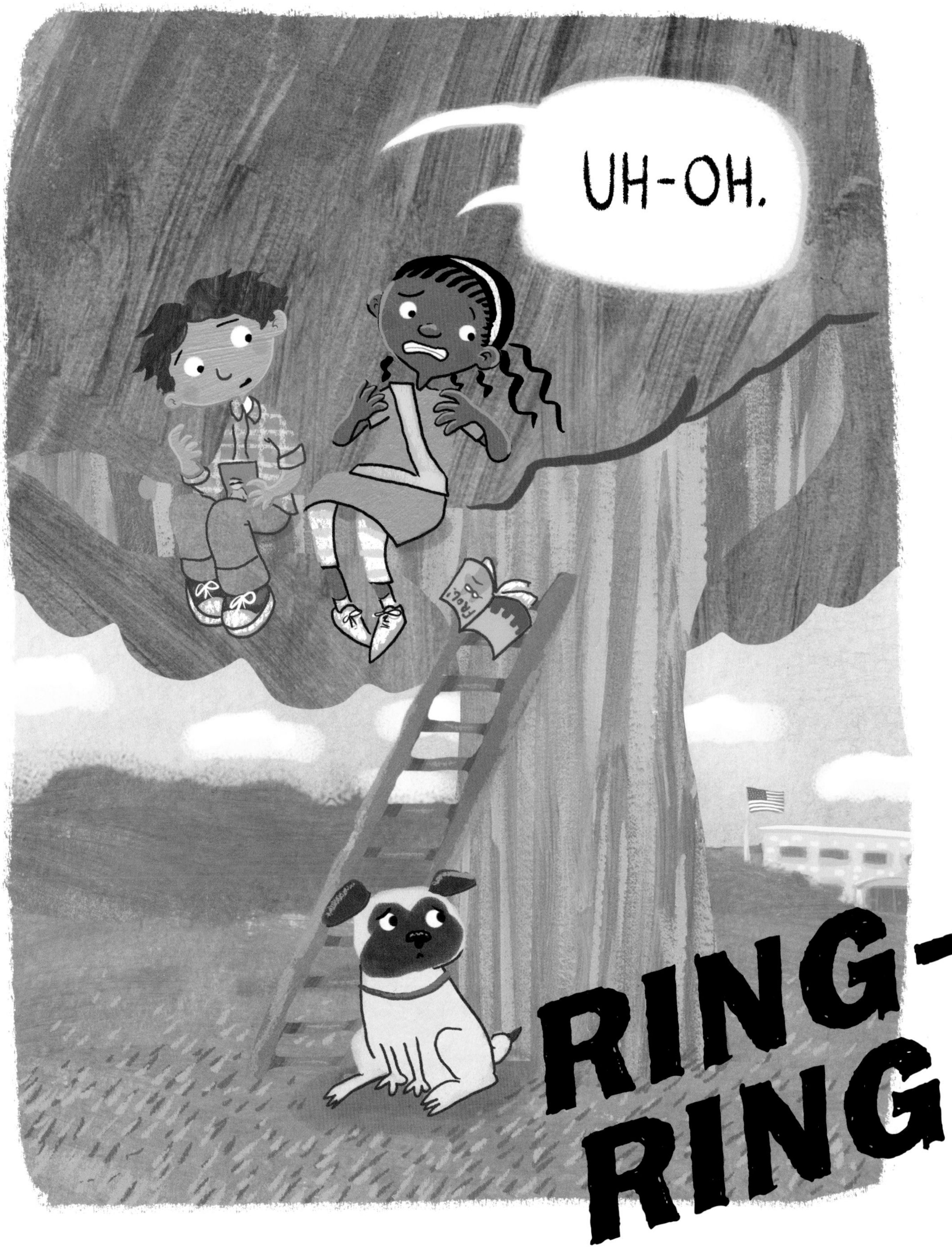
UH-OH.
RING-RING

BOOF!

It was Never-Late Nate.

Never-Late Nate who thought he was sooo great.

So, once again Marty was tardy.

And, yes, so was Never-Late Kate.

A small price to pay for the time to find out
that someone's surprisingly great.

Thursday morning, Marty
bounced out of bed.

He grabbed breakfast to go
and dashed out the door, and
for the first time ever—

Marty was early! Totally early.

On the walk to school, Marty told Kate
about battling giant squids.

And Kate told Marty about using squid
for bait to catch sharks.

Luckily, Marty had brought enough
Toast-on-a-Rope to last the whole way . . .

No matter how long it took.

KATE'S MARTY'S
(Kate's crossed out, Marty's added above)
TOP 5 POINTS
FOR PERPETUAL PUNCTUALITY

1. Select and set out the next day's clothes each night. **Better yet, sleep in them!**

2. Pack your backpack the night before and leave it by the front door. **Where's the spontaneity in that? Besides, I do my best packing in the morning.**

3. Set an alarm. Better yet, set two. **Admit it, you wanted to say three!**

4. Don't hit snooze, Marty! **Who, me?!**

5. Don't skip breakfast! If you're running late, take it with you. **Exactly! Toast-on-a-Rope! Revolutionizing breakfast since Monday!**

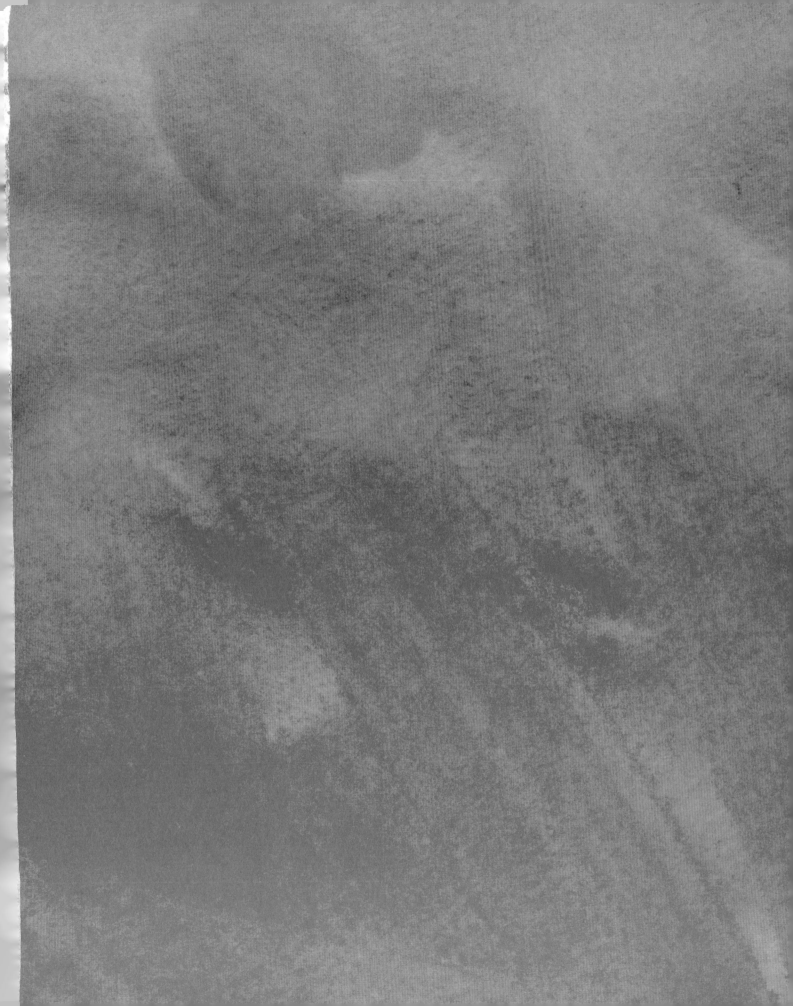